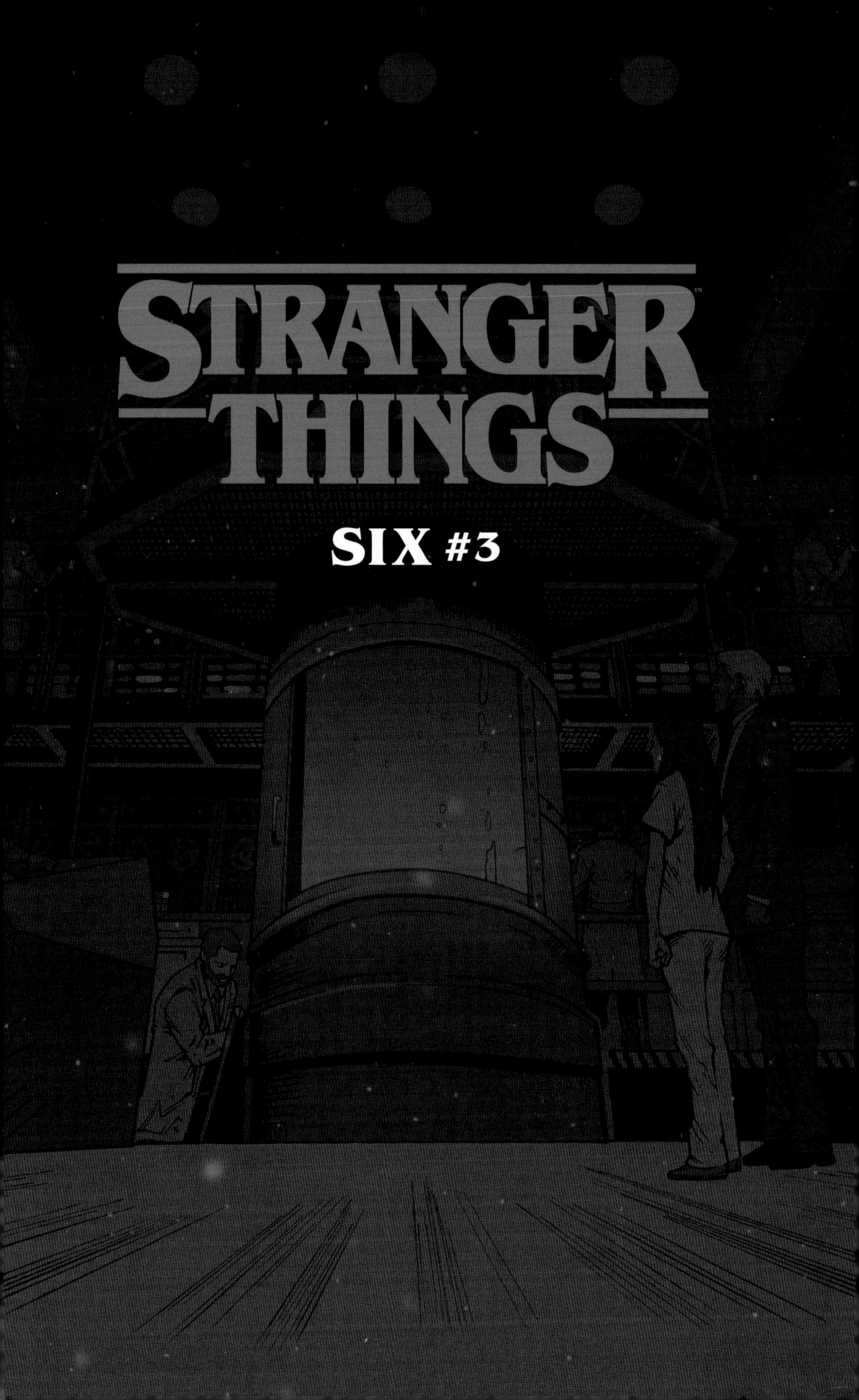
STRANGER THINGS
SIX #3

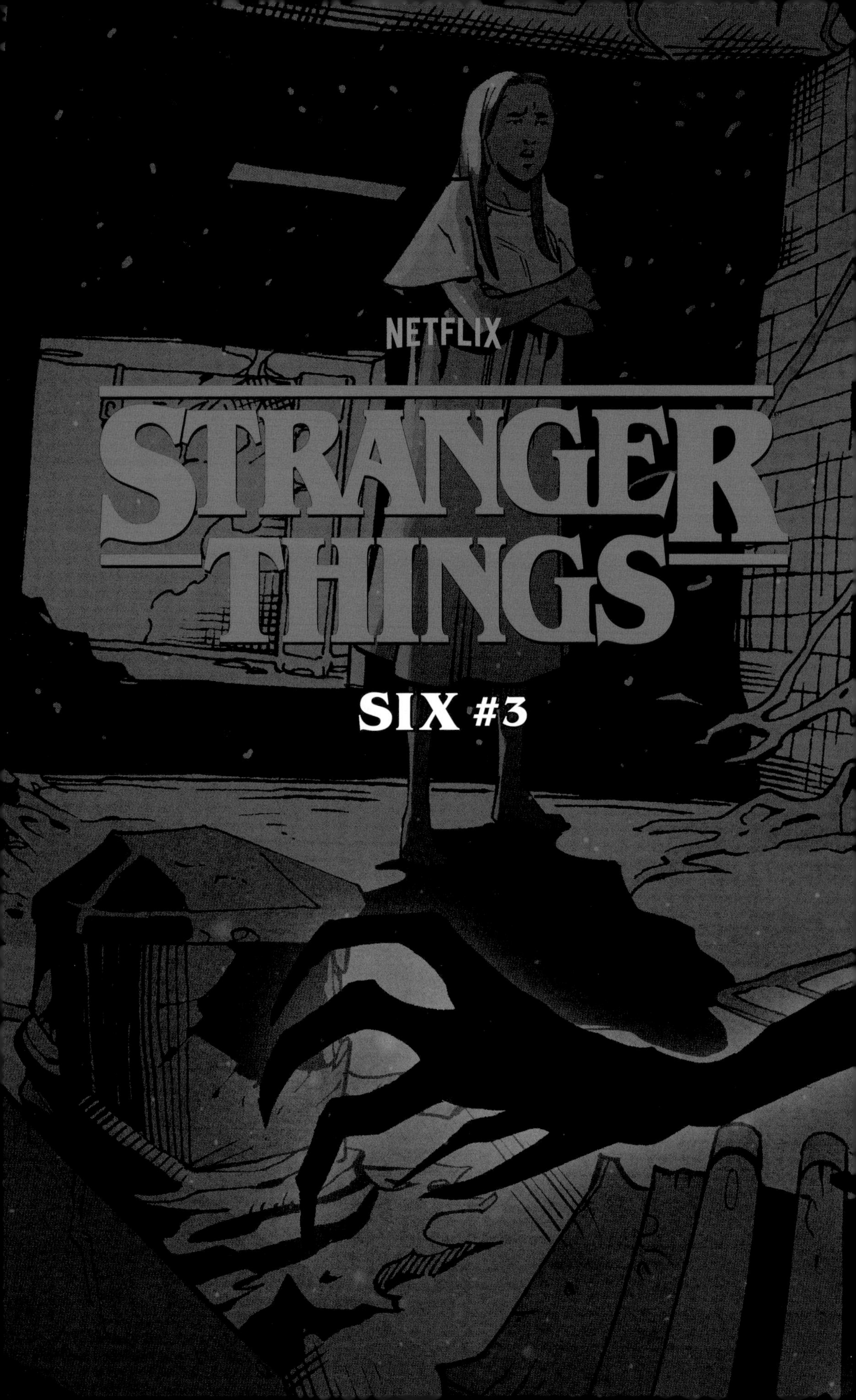
NETFLIX
STRANGER THINGS
SIX #3

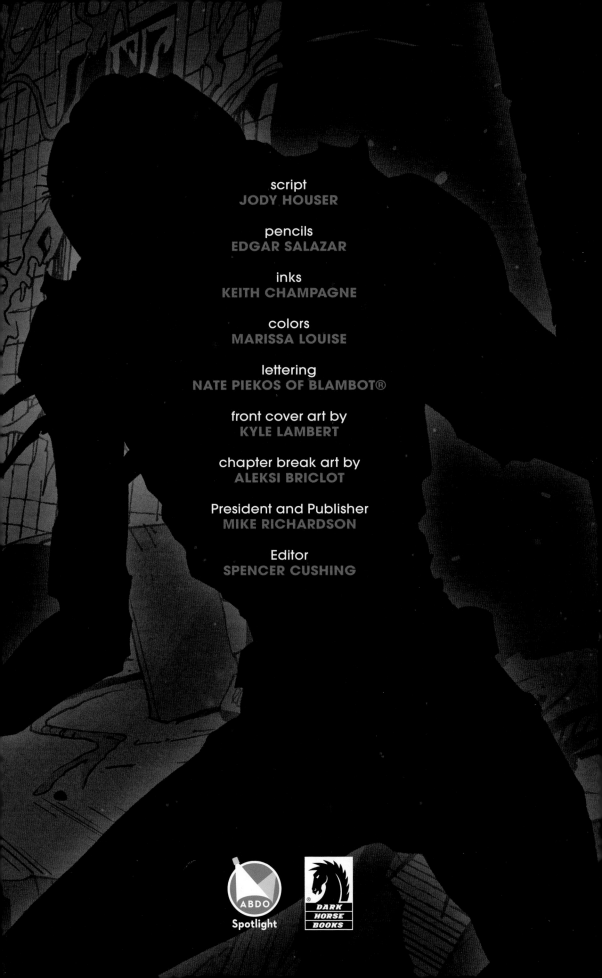

script
JODY HOUSER

pencils
EDGAR SALAZAR

inks
KEITH CHAMPAGNE

colors
MARISSA LOUISE

lettering
NATE PIEKOS OF BLAMBOT®

front cover art by
KYLE LAMBERT

chapter break art by
ALEKSI BRICLOT

President and Publisher
MIKE RICHARDSON

Editor
SPENCER CUSHING

ABDO
Spotlight

DARK
HORSE
BOOKS

Reinforced library bound edition published in 2020 by Spotlight, a division of ABDO, PO Box 398166, Minneapolis, Minnesota 55439. Spotlight produces high-quality reinforced library bound editions for schools and libraries.
Published by agreement with Dark Horse Comics.

Printed in the United States of America, North Mankato, Minnesota.
092019
012020

THIS BOOK CONTAINS
RECYCLED MATERIALS

NETFLIX
OFFICIAL MERCHANDISE
©NETFLIX

Library of Congress Control Number: 2019942387

Publisher's Cataloging-in-Publication Data

Names: Houser, Jody, author. | Salazar, Edgar; Champagne, Keith; Louise, Marissa; Piekos, Nate, illustrators.
Title: Six / by Jody Houser; illustrated by Edgar Salazar; Keith Champagne; Marissa Louise; Nate Piekos.
Description: Minneapolis, Minnesota : Spotlight, 2020 | Series: Stranger things
Summary: A teenage girl with precognitive abilities ends up as the pawn of a government agency that wants to harness her powers for its own ends.
Identifiers: ISBN 9781532144400 (#1, lib. bdg.) | ISBN 9781532144417 (#2, lib. bdg.) | ISBN 9781532144424 (#3, lib. bdg.) | ISBN 9781532144431 (#4, lib. bdg.)
Subjects: LCSH: Stranger things (Television program)--Juvenile fiction. | Science fiction television programs--Juvenile fiction. | Supernatural disappearances--Juvenile fiction. | Monsters--Juvenile fiction. | Graphic novels--Juvenile fiction. | Comic books, strips, etc.--Juvenile fiction.
Classification: DDC 741.5--dc23

Spotlight

A Division of ABDO
abdobooks.com

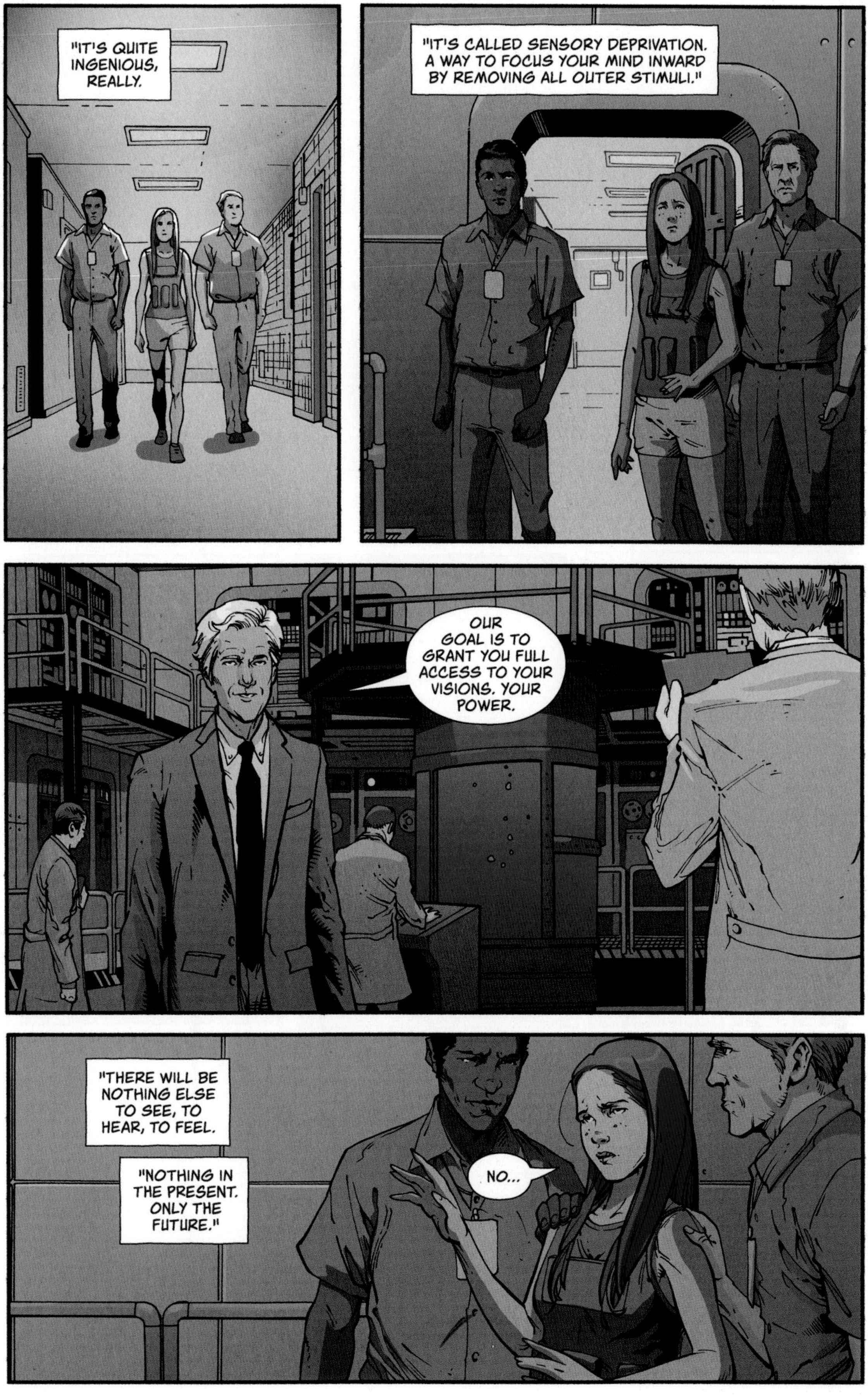
"IT'S QUITE INGENIOUS, REALLY.
"IT'S CALLED SENSORY DEPRIVATION. A WAY TO FOCUS YOUR MIND INWARD BY REMOVING ALL OUTER STIMULI."
OUR GOAL IS TO GRANT YOU FULL ACCESS TO YOUR VISIONS. YOUR POWER.
"THERE WILL BE NOTHING ELSE TO SEE, TO HEAR, TO FEEL.
"NOTHING IN THE PRESENT. ONLY THE FUTURE."
NO...

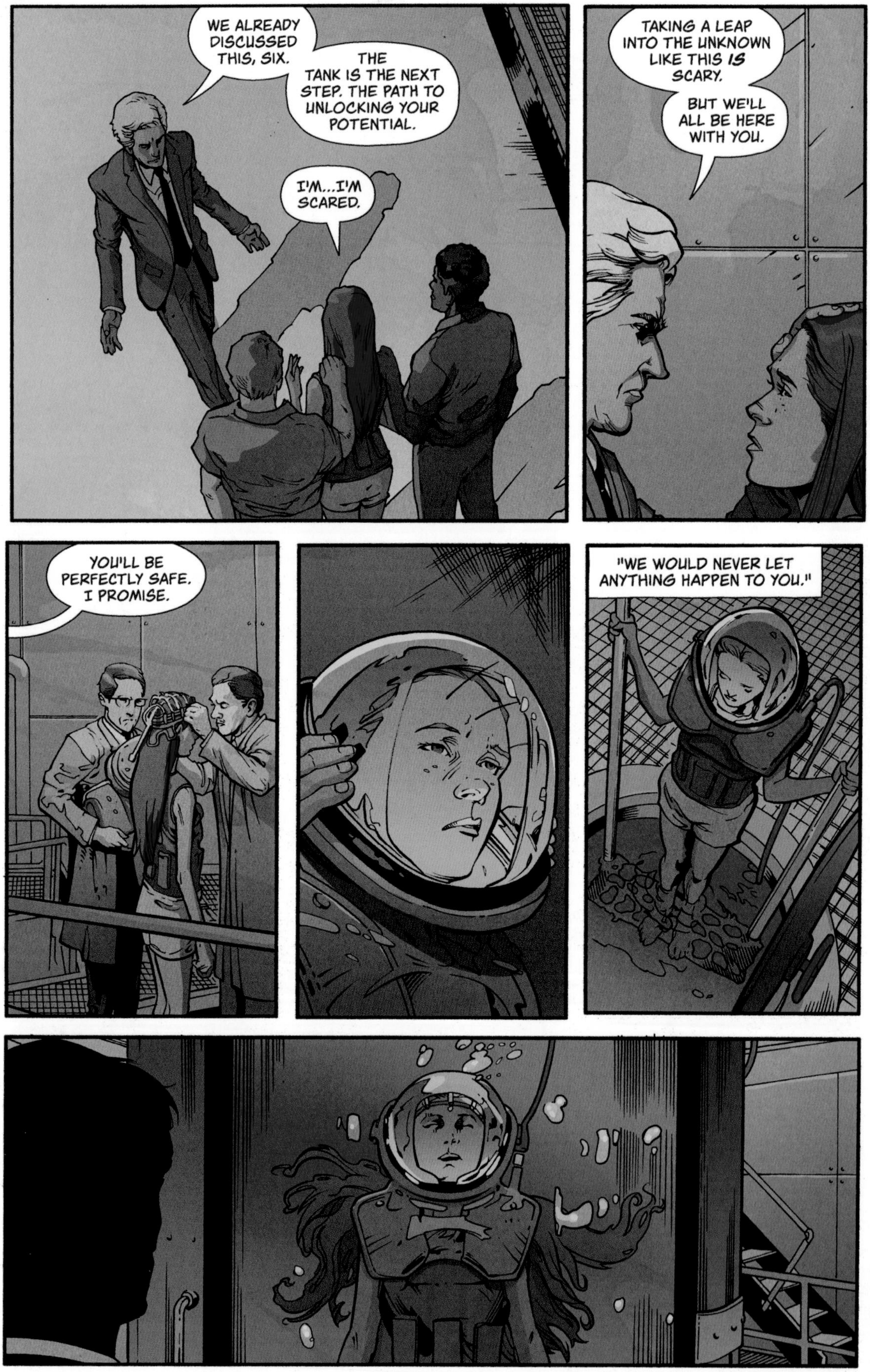
WE ALREADY DISCUSSED THIS, SIX.
THE TANK IS THE NEXT STEP. THE PATH TO UNLOCKING YOUR POTENTIAL.
I'M...I'M SCARED.
TAKING A LEAP INTO THE UNKNOWN LIKE THIS *IS* SCARY.
BUT WE'LL ALL BE HERE WITH YOU.
YOU'LL BE PERFECTLY SAFE. I PROMISE.
"WE WOULD NEVER LET ANYTHING HAPPEN TO YOU."

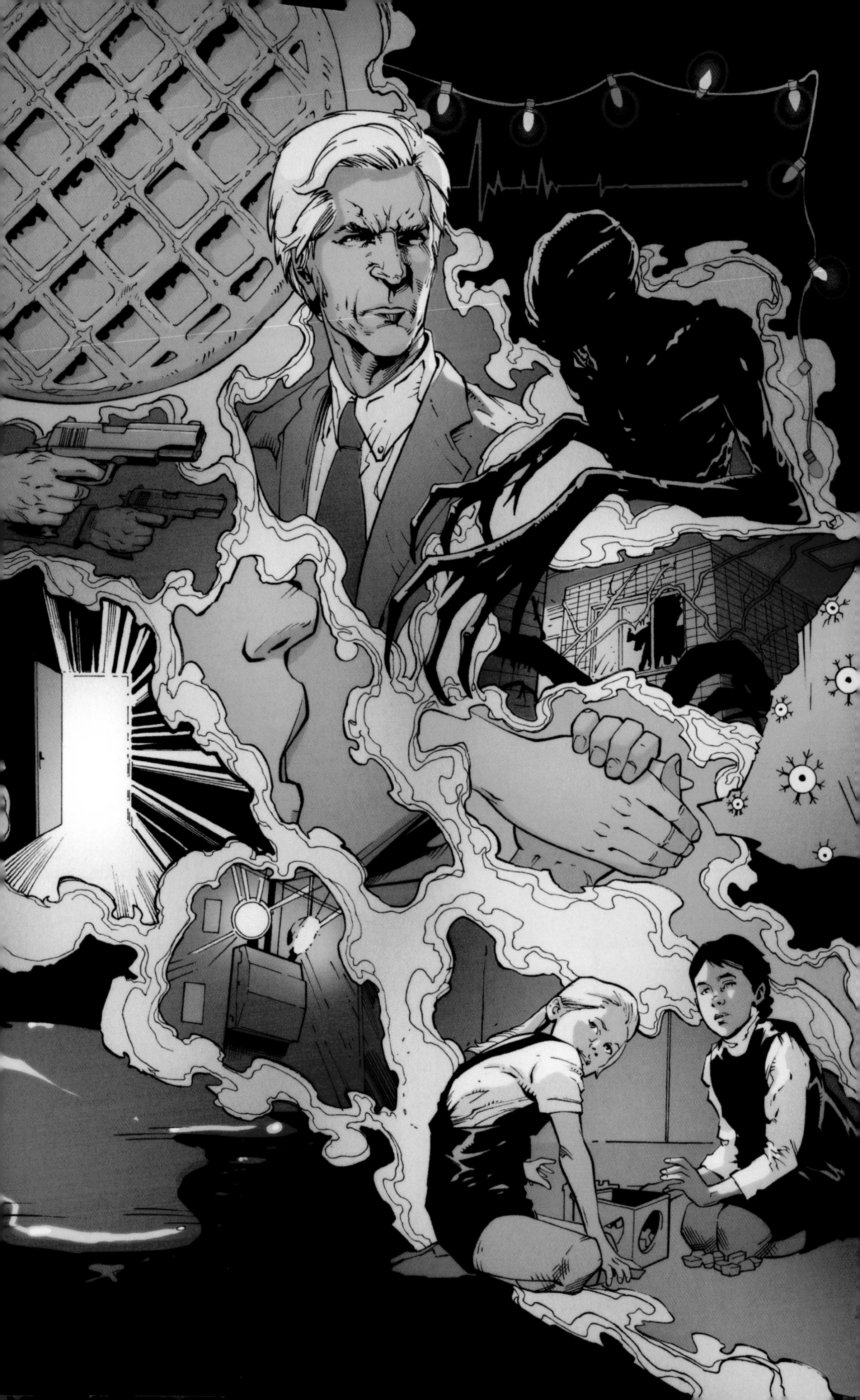

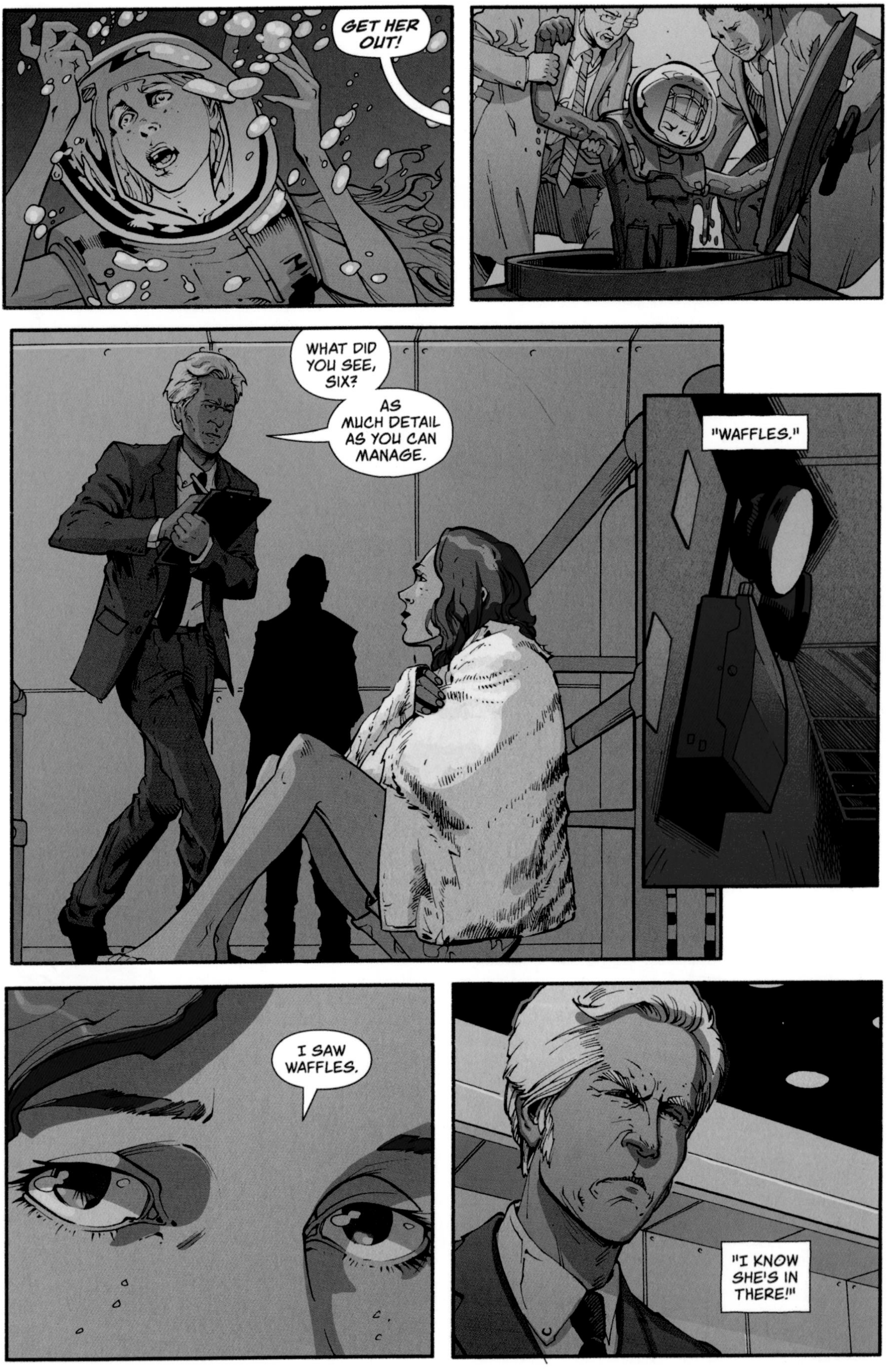
GET HER OUT!
WHAT DID YOU SEE, SIX?
AS MUCH DETAIL AS YOU CAN MANAGE.
"WAFFLES."
I SAW WAFFLES.
"I KNOW SHE'S IN THERE!"

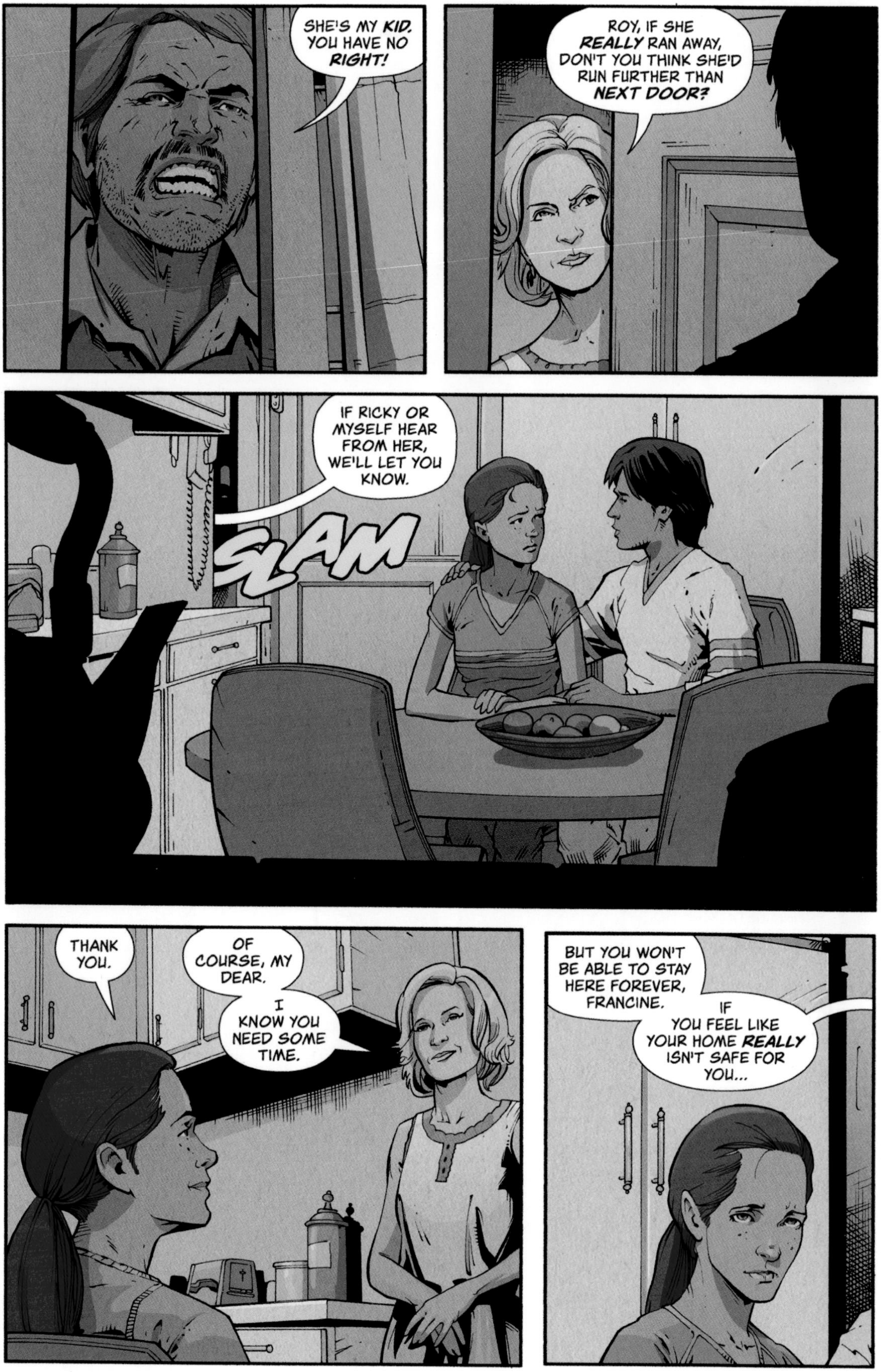
SHE'S MY KID. YOU HAVE NO RIGHT!
ROY, IF SHE REALLY RAN AWAY, DON'T YOU THINK SHE'D RUN FURTHER THAN NEXT DOOR?
IF RICKY OR MYSELF HEAR FROM HER, WE'LL LET YOU KNOW.
SLAM
THANK YOU.
OF COURSE, MY DEAR.
I KNOW YOU NEED SOME TIME.
BUT YOU WON'T BE ABLE TO STAY HERE FOREVER, FRANCINE.
IF YOU FEEL LIKE YOUR HOME REALLY ISN'T SAFE FOR YOU...

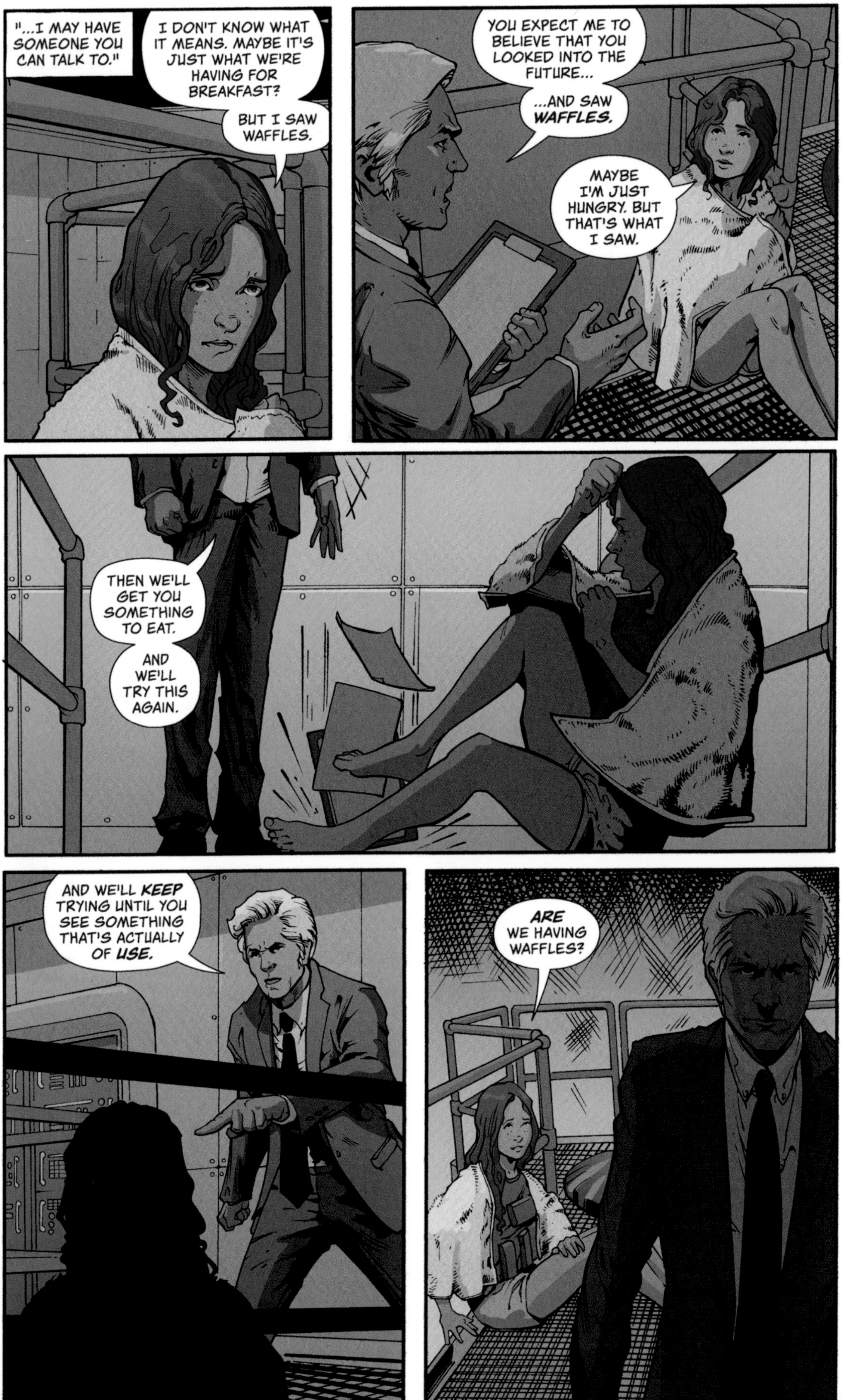
"...I MAY HAVE SOMEONE YOU CAN TALK TO."
I DON'T KNOW WHAT IT MEANS. MAYBE IT'S JUST WHAT WE'RE HAVING FOR BREAKFAST?
BUT I SAW WAFFLES.
YOU EXPECT ME TO BELIEVE THAT YOU LOOKED INTO THE FUTURE...
...AND SAW *WAFFLES.*
MAYBE I'M JUST HUNGRY. BUT THAT'S WHAT I SAW.
THEN WE'LL GET YOU SOMETHING TO EAT.
AND WE'LL TRY THIS AGAIN.
AND WE'LL *KEEP* TRYING UNTIL YOU SEE SOMETHING THAT'S ACTUALLY OF *USE.*
ARE WE HAVING WAFFLES?

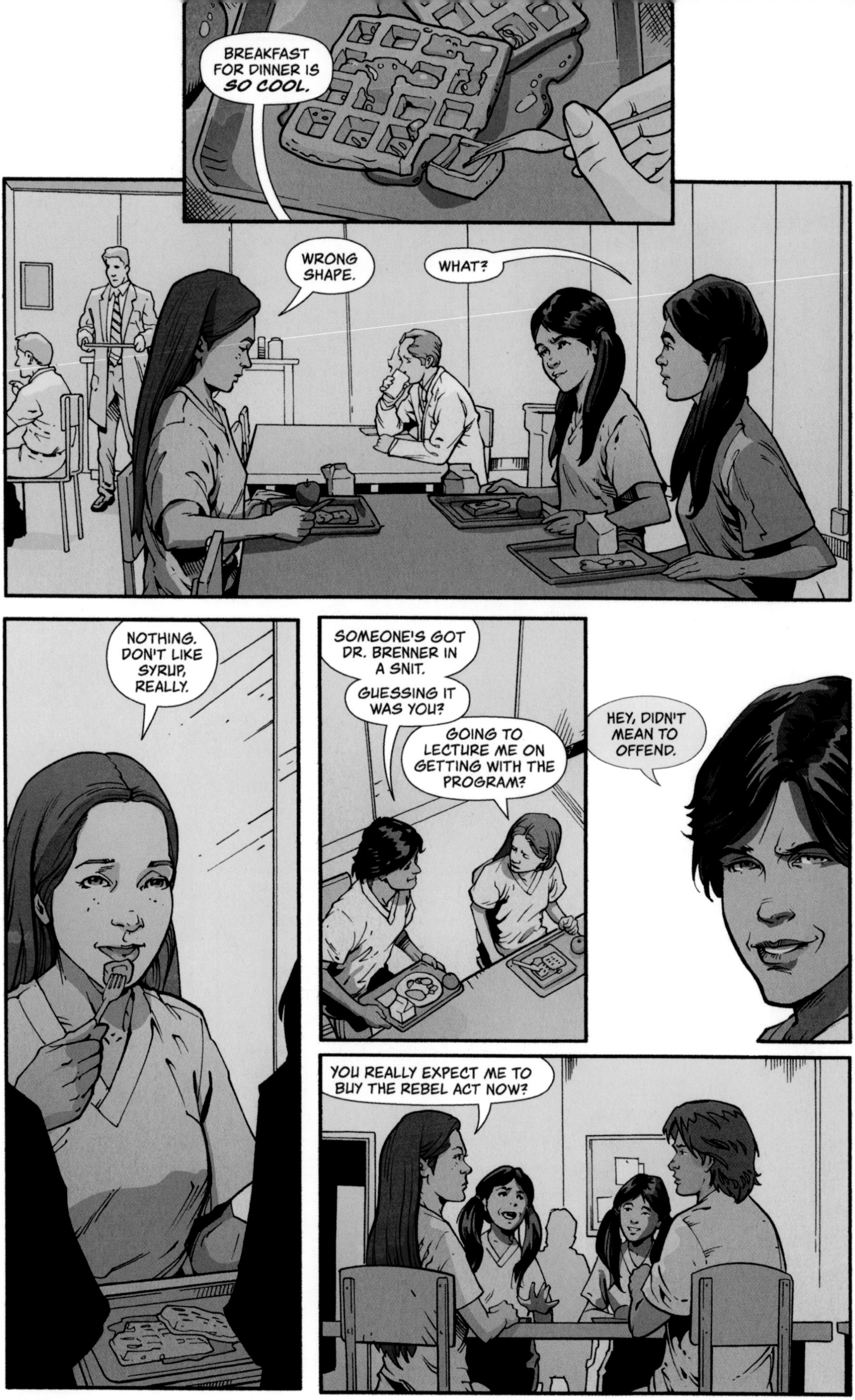
BREAKFAST FOR DINNER IS SO COOL.
WRONG SHAPE.
WHAT?
NOTHING. DON'T LIKE SYRUP, REALLY.
SOMEONE'S GOT DR. BRENNER IN A SNIT.
GUESSING IT WAS YOU?
GOING TO LECTURE ME ON GETTING WITH THE PROGRAM?
HEY, DIDN'T MEAN TO OFFEND.
YOU REALLY EXPECT ME TO BUY THE REBEL ACT NOW?

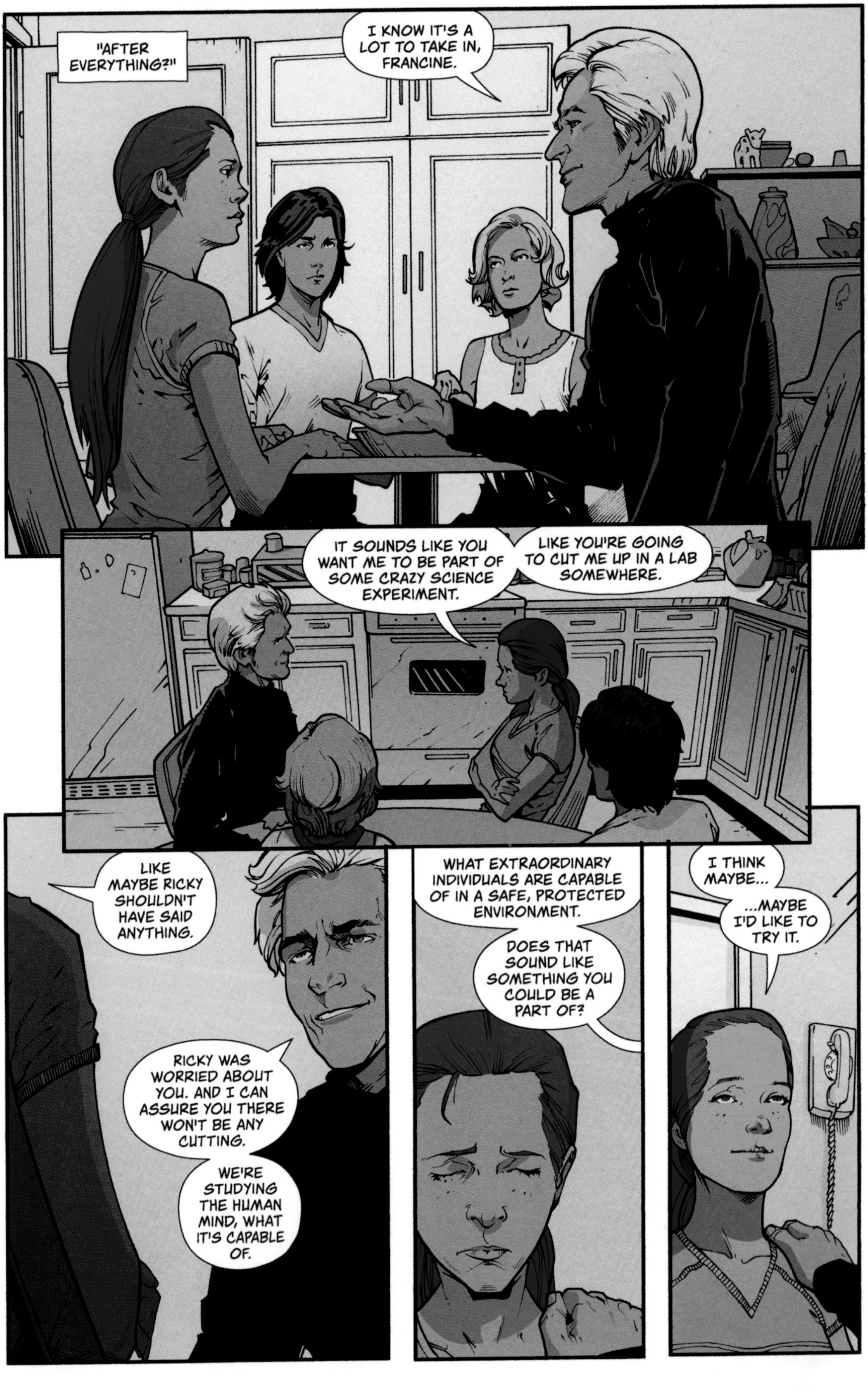
"AFTER EVERYTHING?!"
I KNOW IT'S A LOT TO TAKE IN, FRANCINE.
IT SOUNDS LIKE YOU WANT ME TO BE PART OF SOME CRAZY SCIENCE EXPERIMENT.
LIKE YOU'RE GOING TO CUT ME UP IN A LAB SOMEWHERE.
LIKE MAYBE RICKY SHOULDN'T HAVE SAID ANYTHING.
RICKY WAS WORRIED ABOUT YOU. AND I CAN ASSURE YOU THERE WON'T BE ANY CUTTING.
WE'RE STUDYING THE HUMAN MIND, WHAT IT'S CAPABLE OF.
WHAT EXTRAORDINARY INDIVIDUALS ARE CAPABLE OF IN A SAFE, PROTECTED ENVIRONMENT.
DOES THAT SOUND LIKE SOMETHING YOU COULD BE A PART OF?
I THINK MAYBE...
...MAYBE I'D LIKE TO TRY IT.

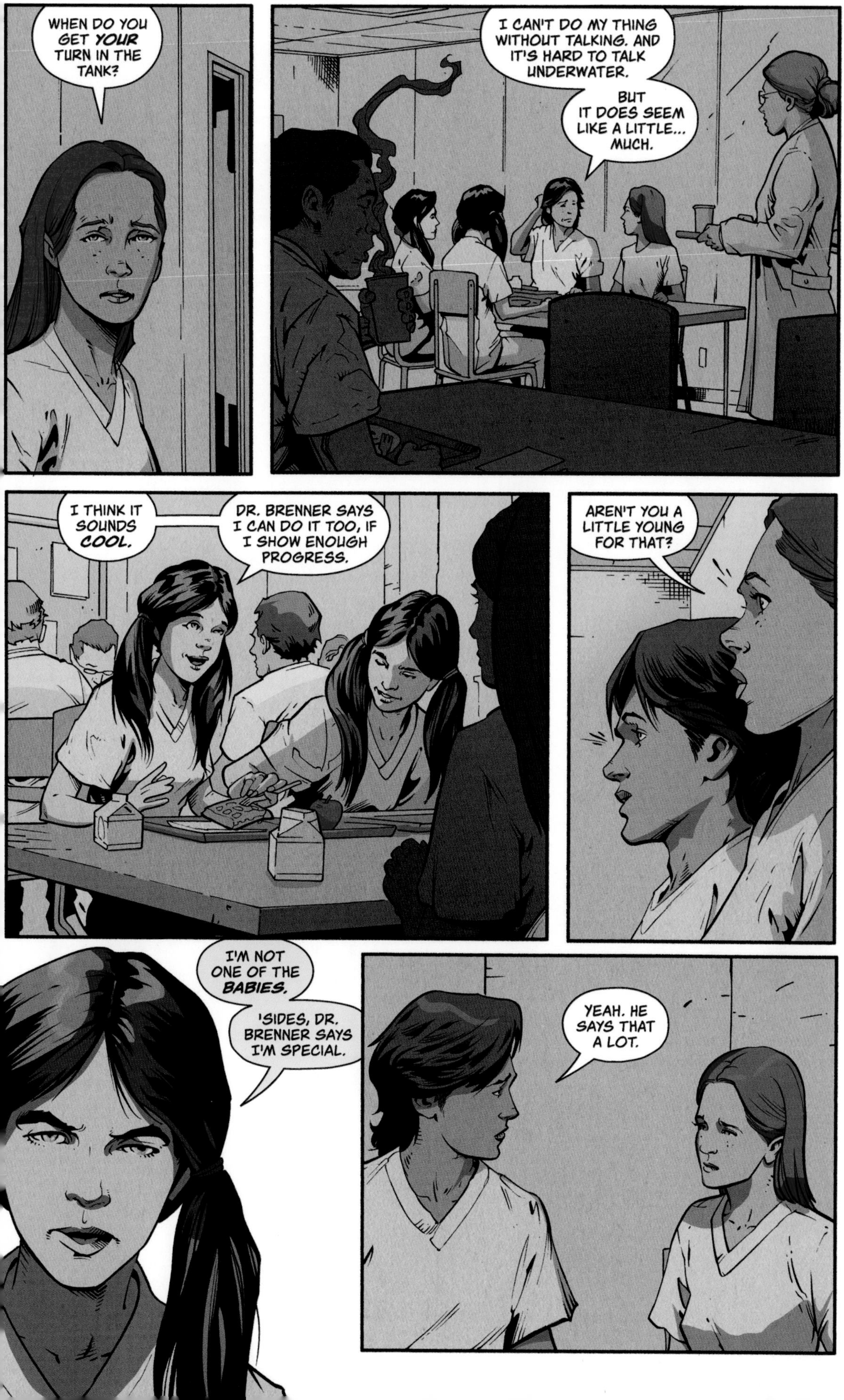
WHEN DO YOU GET YOUR TURN IN THE TANK?
I CAN'T DO MY THING WITHOUT TALKING. AND IT'S HARD TO TALK UNDERWATER.
BUT IT DOES SEEM LIKE A LITTLE... MUCH.
I THINK IT SOUNDS COOL.
DR. BRENNER SAYS I CAN DO IT TOO, IF I SHOW ENOUGH PROGRESS.
AREN'T YOU A LITTLE YOUNG FOR THAT?
I'M NOT ONE OF THE BABIES.
'SIDES, DR. BRENNER SAYS I'M SPECIAL.
YEAH. HE SAYS THAT A LOT.

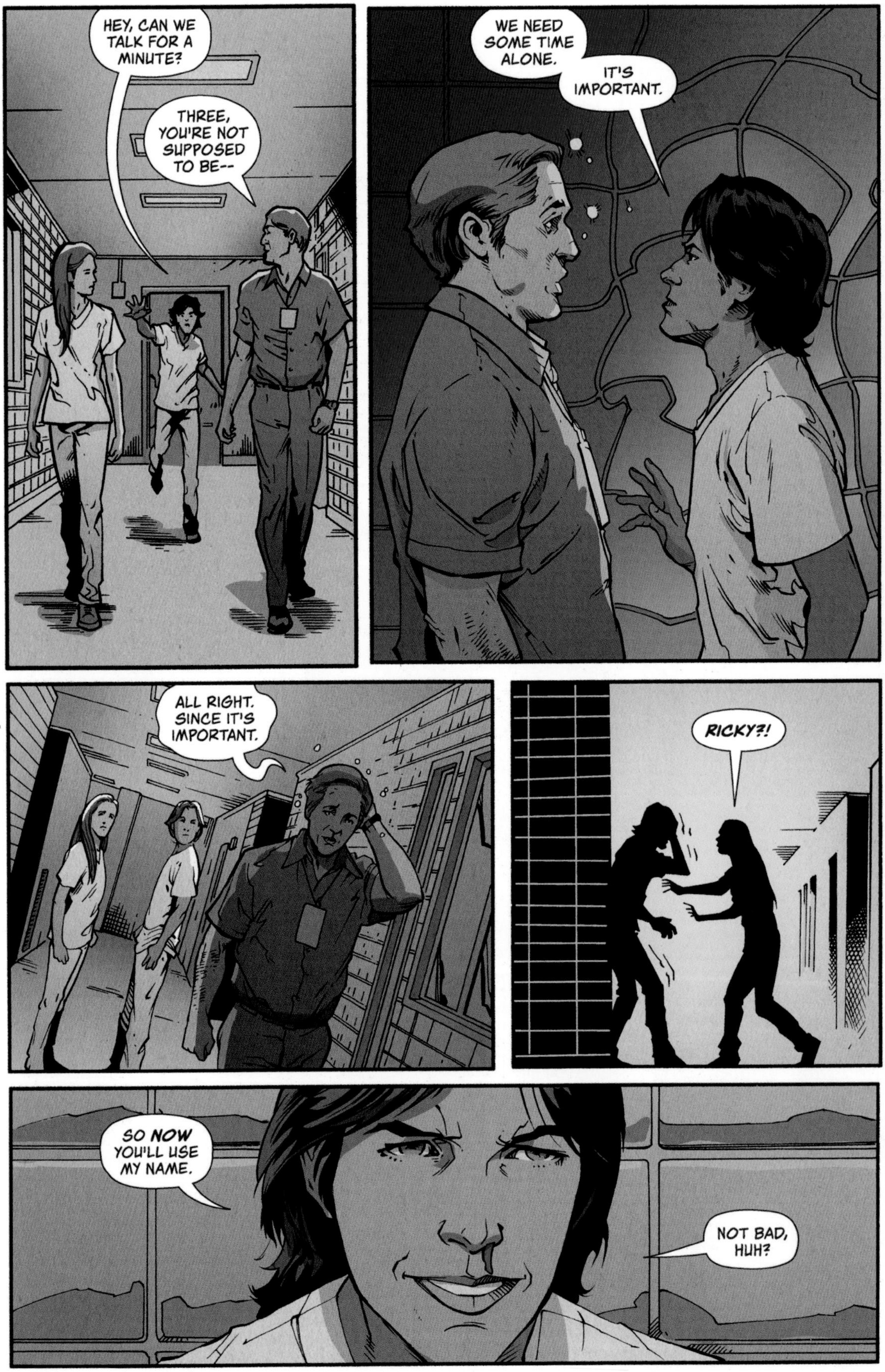
HEY, CAN WE TALK FOR A MINUTE?
THREE, YOU'RE NOT SUPPOSED TO BE--
WE NEED SOME TIME ALONE.
IT'S IMPORTANT.
ALL RIGHT. SINCE IT'S IMPORTANT.
RICKY?!
SO NOW YOU'LL USE MY NAME.
NOT BAD, HUH?

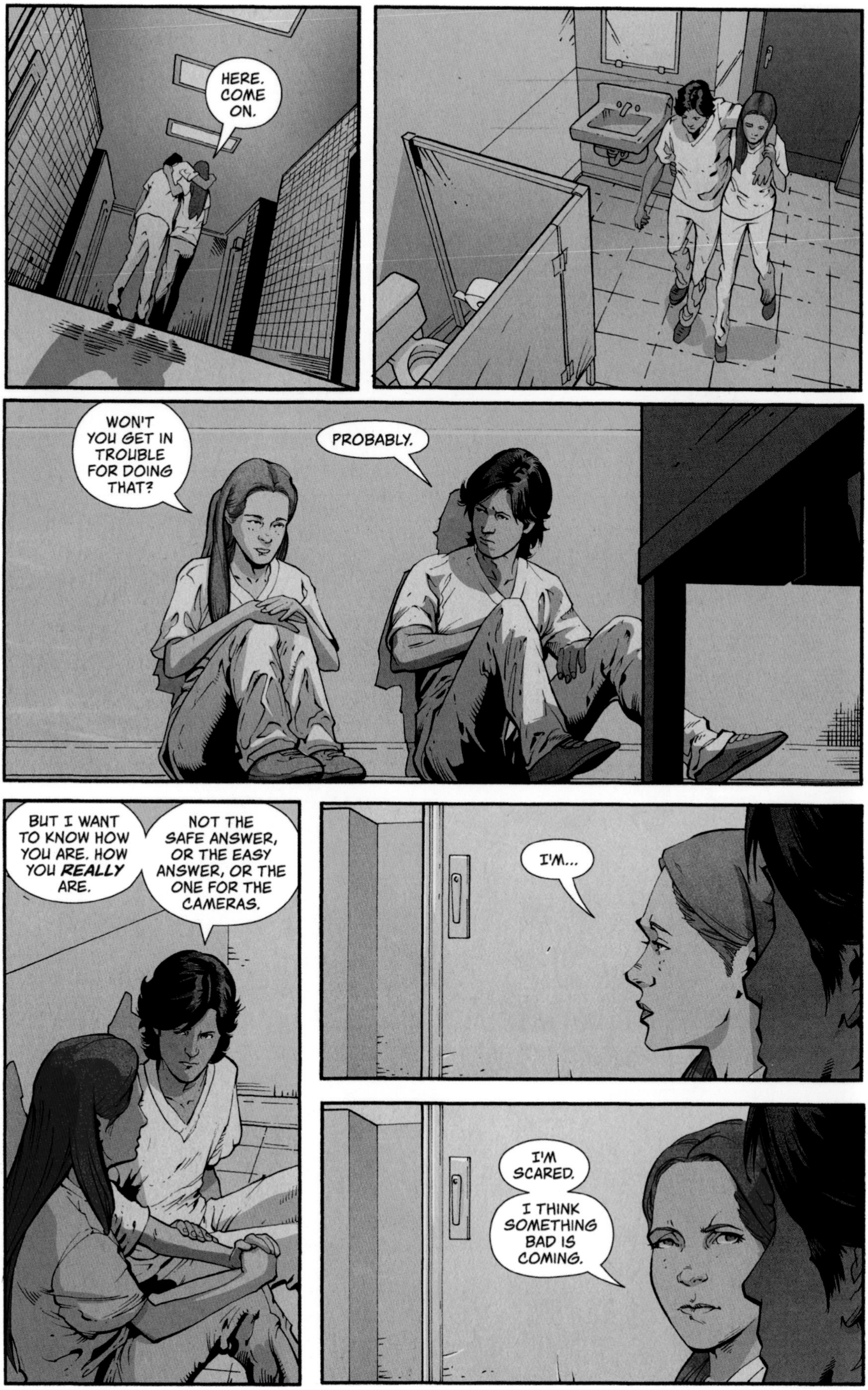
HERE. COME ON.
WON'T YOU GET IN TROUBLE FOR DOING THAT?
PROBABLY.
BUT I WANT TO KNOW HOW YOU ARE. HOW YOU *REALLY* ARE.
NOT THE SAFE ANSWER, OR THE EASY ANSWER, OR THE ONE FOR THE CAMERAS.
I'M...
I'M SCARED.
I THINK SOMETHING BAD IS COMING.

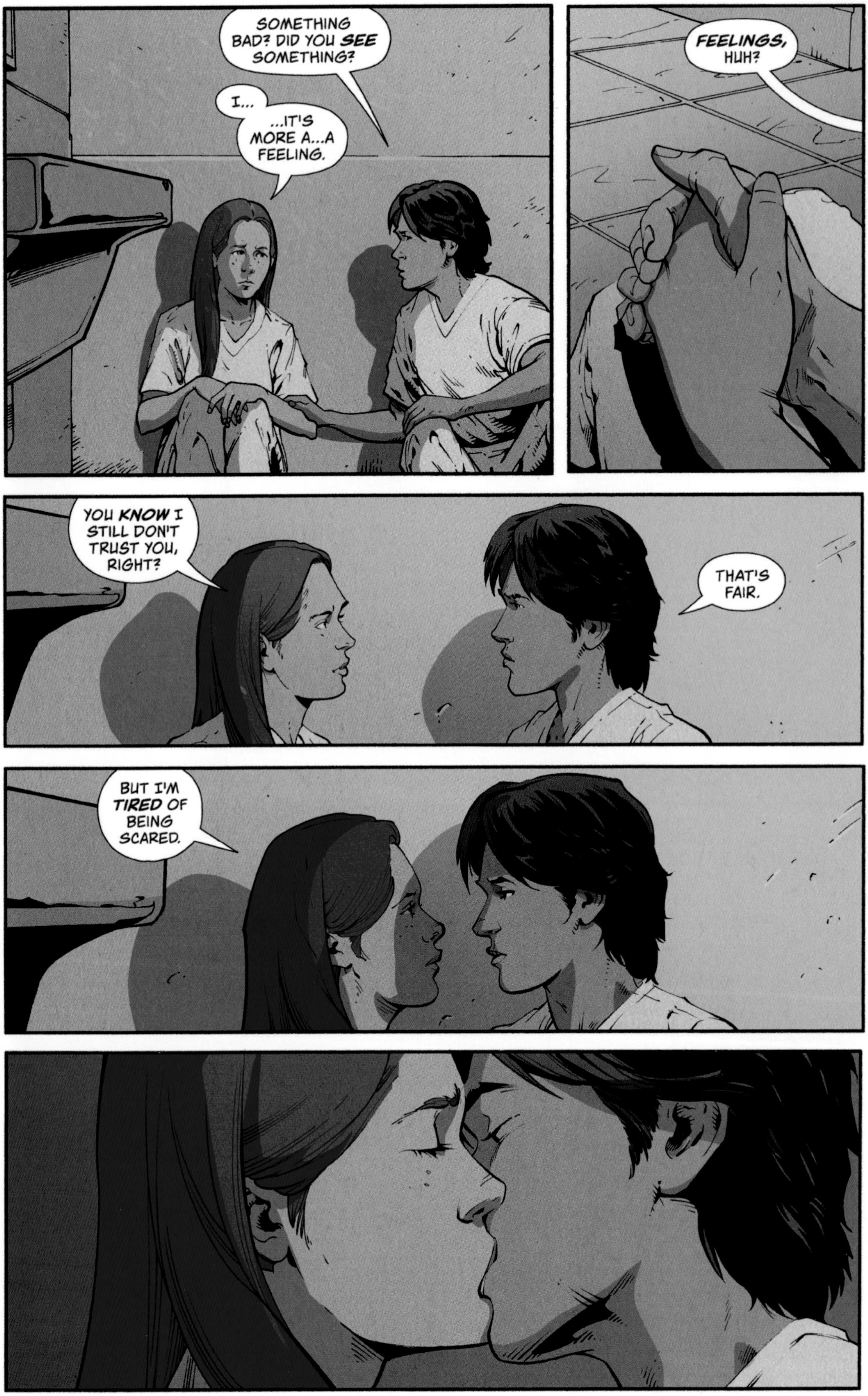
SOMETHING BAD? DID YOU SEE SOMETHING?
I...
...IT'S MORE A...A FEELING.
FEELINGS, HUH?
YOU KNOW I STILL DON'T TRUST YOU, RIGHT?
THAT'S FAIR.
BUT I'M TIRED OF BEING SCARED.

"SO WHY EXACTLY ARE WE WATCHING THIS?"

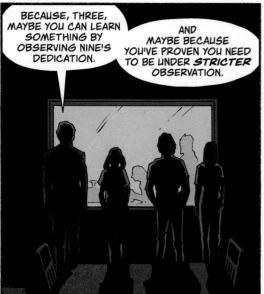

BECAUSE, THREE, MAYBE YOU CAN LEARN SOMETHING BY OBSERVING NINE'S DEDICATION.

AND MAYBE BECAUSE YOU'VE PROVEN YOU NEED TO BE UNDER *STRICTER* OBSERVATION.

WHY DON'T I GET TO BE WITH HER THIS TIME?

WE'RE TRYING SOMETHING NEW FOR THIS SESSION.

"THE MATERIAL THAT NINE IS TRYING TO HEAT HAS BEEN DOUSED WITH A FLAMMABLE LIQUID.

"FOR NOW, WE'LL BE OBSERVING FROM HERE."

ISN'T THAT DANGEROUS?

IF NINE HAD EVER ACHIEVED ANYTHING *CLOSE* TO THE AUTOIGNITION TEMPERATURE NEEDED, PERHAPS.

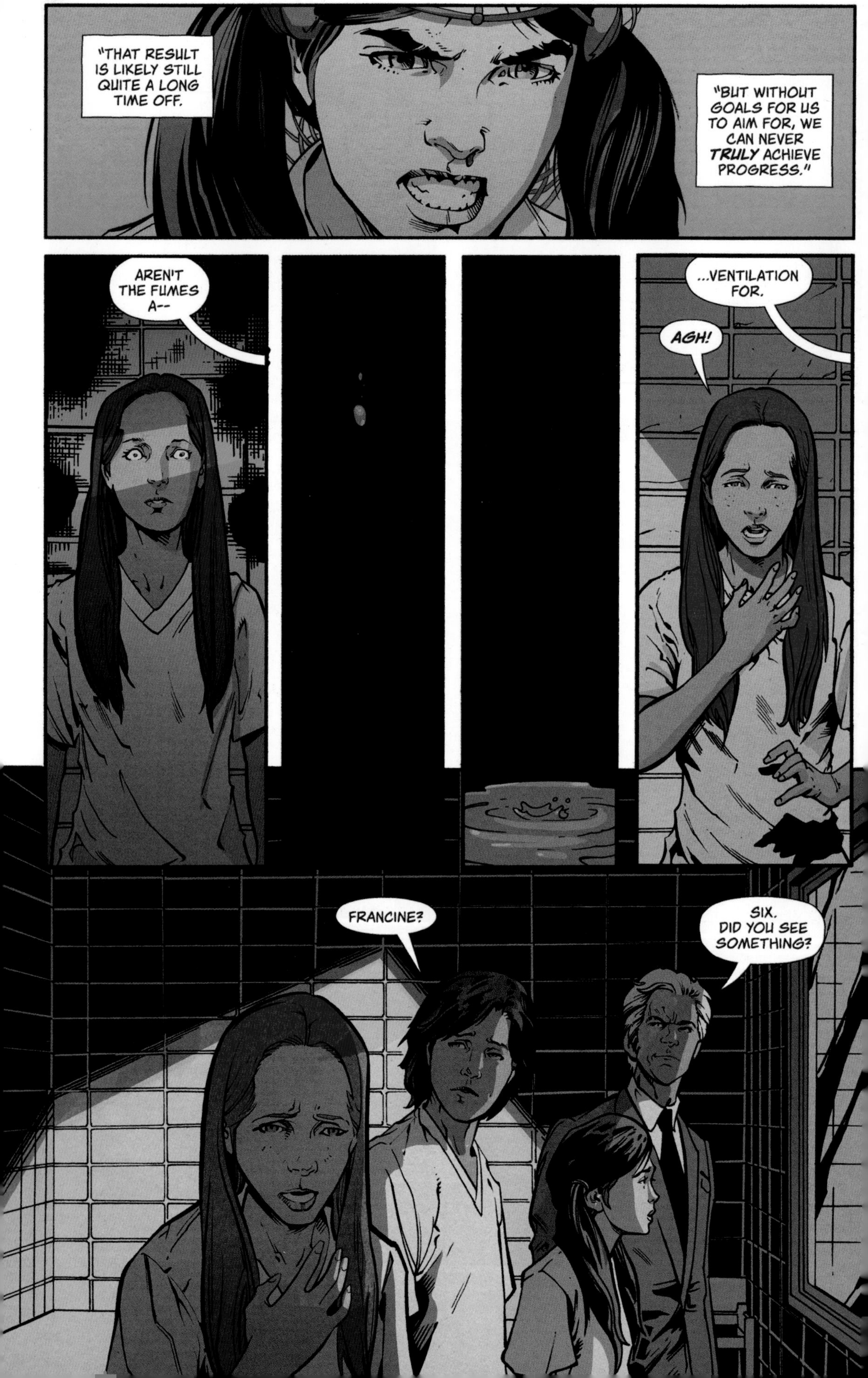
"THAT RESULT IS LIKELY STILL QUITE A LONG TIME OFF.
"BUT WITHOUT GOALS FOR US TO AIM FOR, WE CAN NEVER *TRULY* ACHIEVE PROGRESS."
AREN'T THE FUMES A--
...VENTILATION FOR.
AGH!
FRANCINE?
SIX. DID YOU SEE SOMETHING?

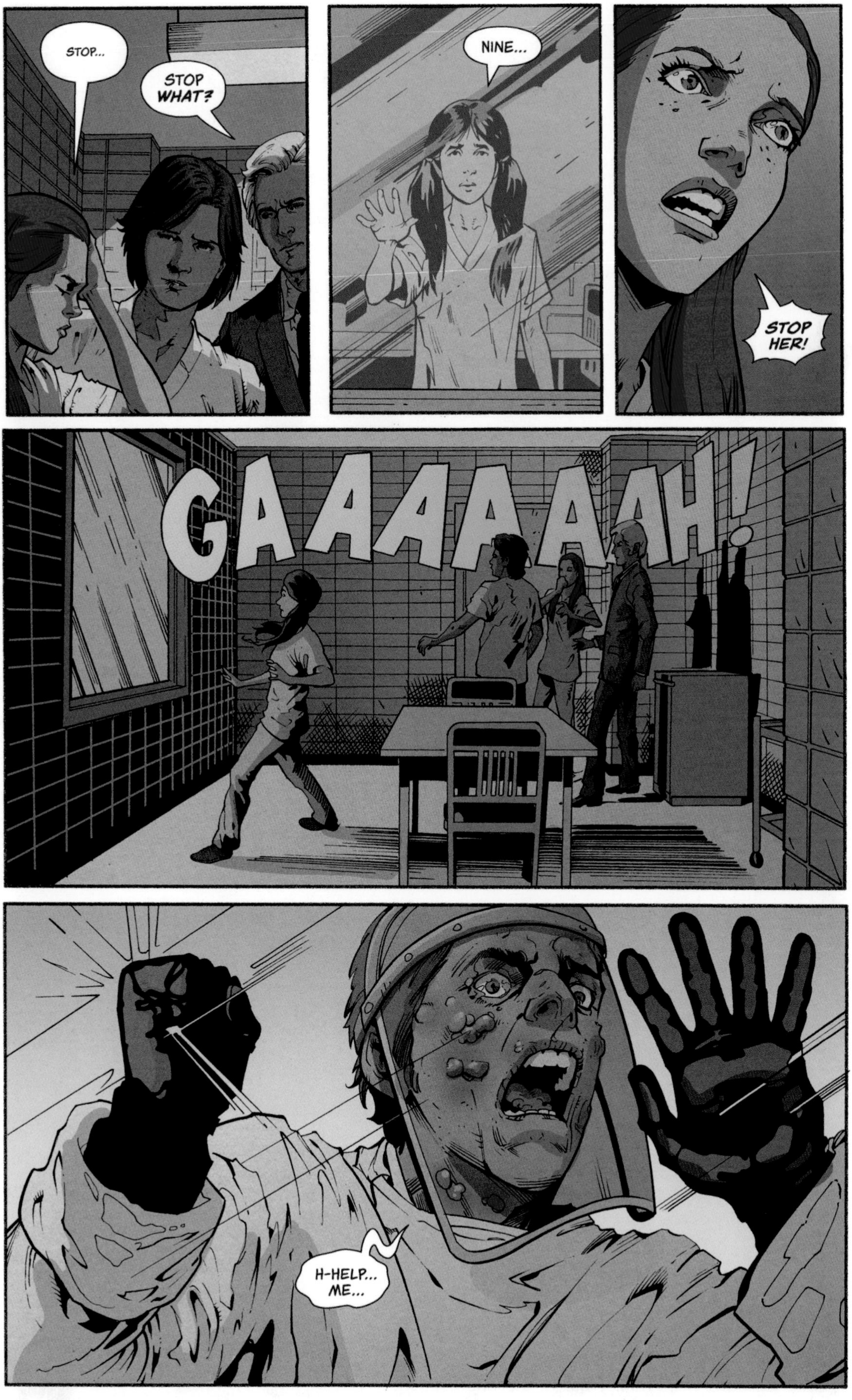
STOP...
STOP WHAT?
NINE...
STOP HER!
GAAAAAAH!
H-HELP... ME...

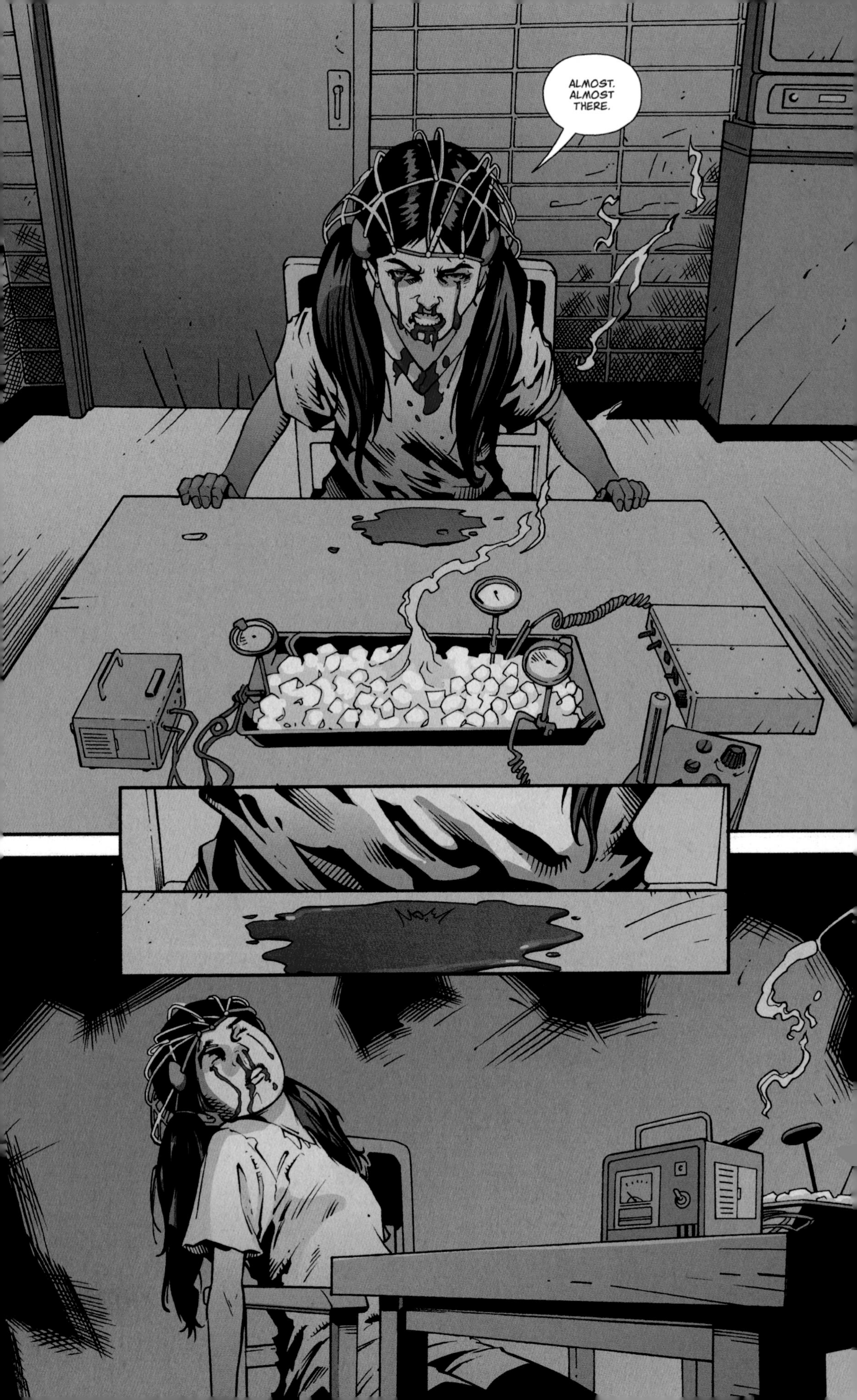
ALMOST. ALMOST THERE.

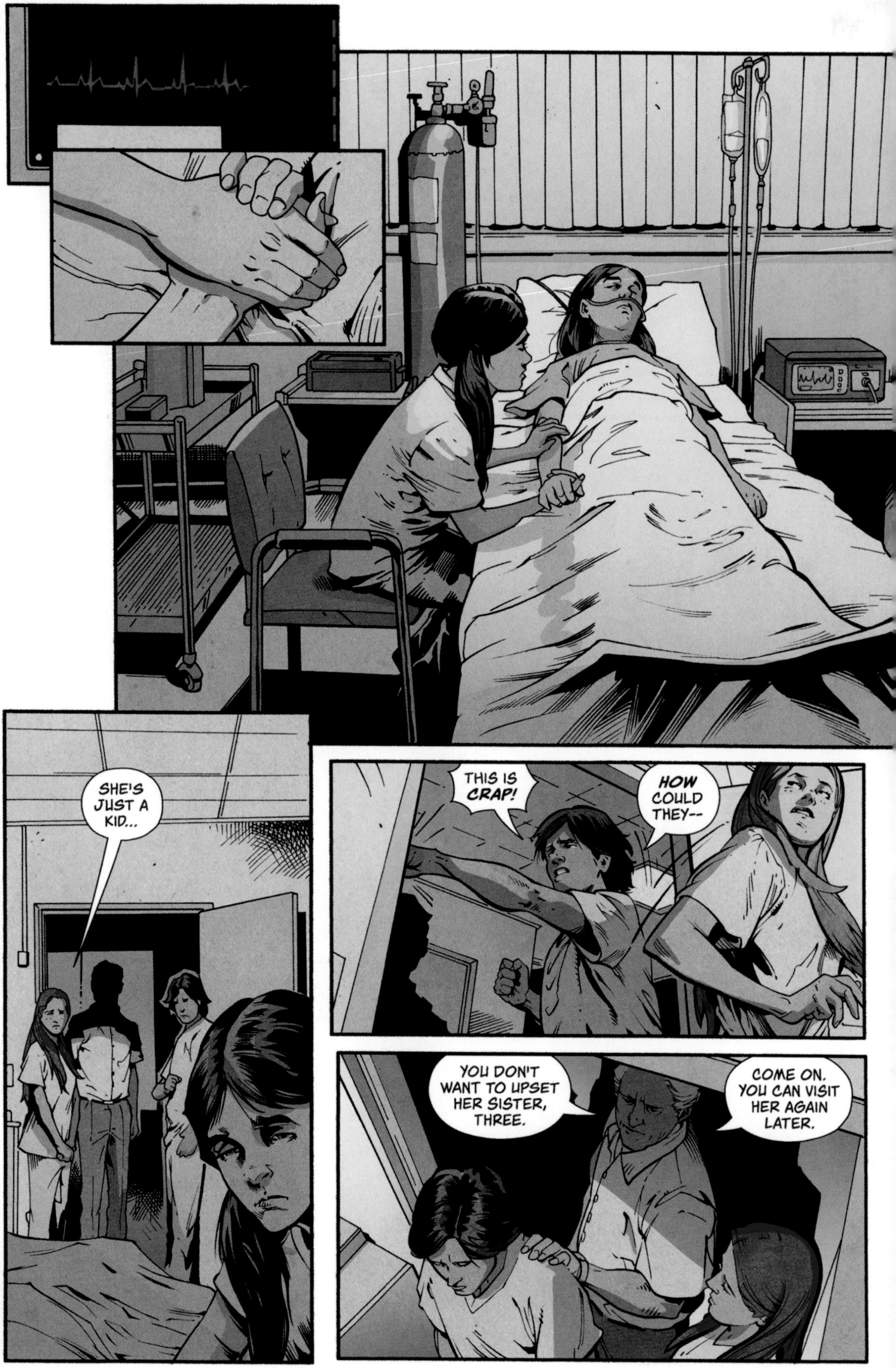
SHE'S JUST A KID...
THIS IS CRAP!
HOW COULD THEY--
YOU DON'T WANT TO UPSET HER SISTER, THREE.
COME ON. YOU CAN VISIT HER AGAIN LATER.

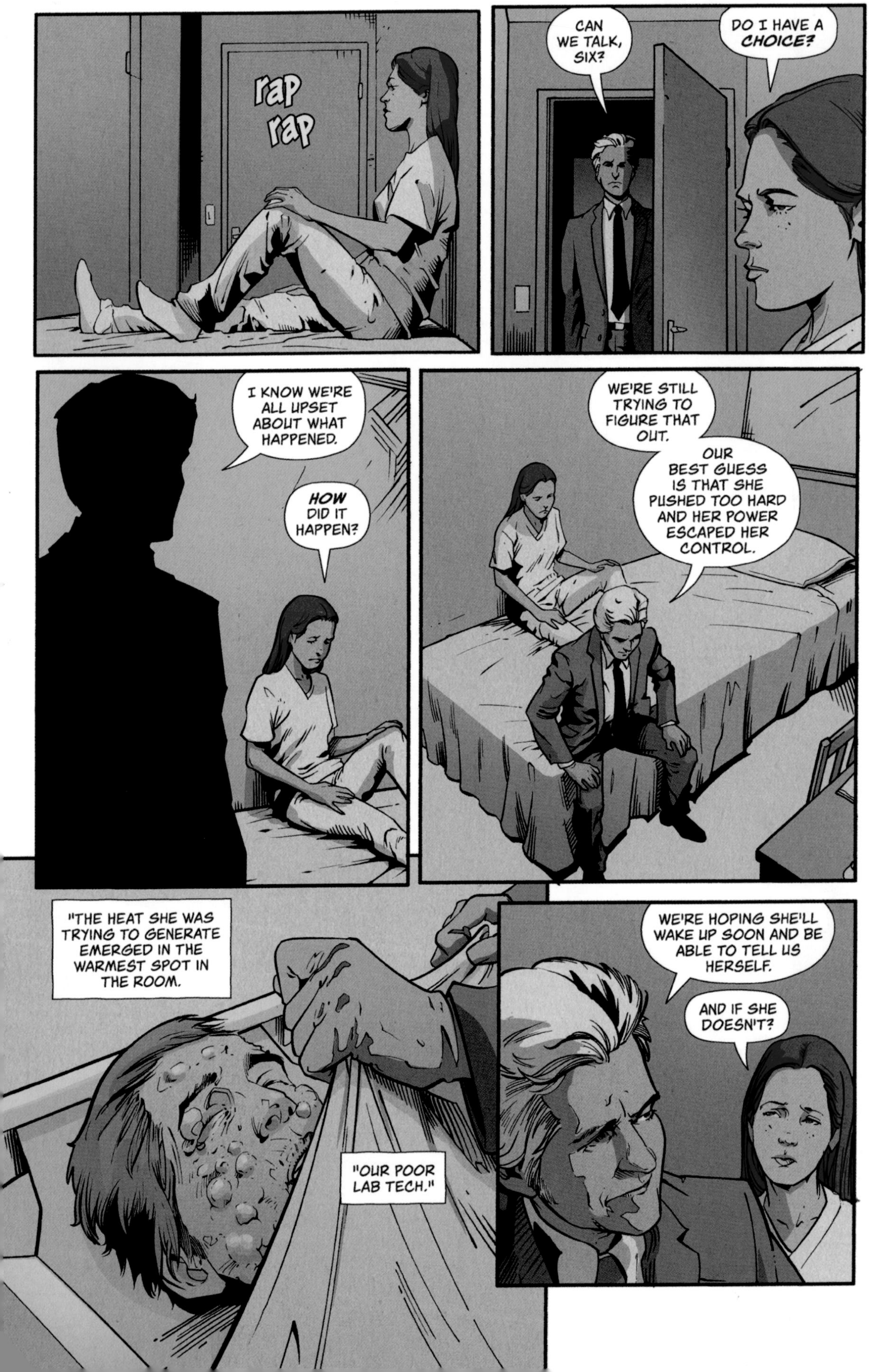
rap rap
CAN WE TALK, SIX?
DO I HAVE A CHOICE?
I KNOW WE'RE ALL UPSET ABOUT WHAT HAPPENED.
HOW DID IT HAPPEN?
WE'RE STILL TRYING TO FIGURE THAT OUT.
OUR BEST GUESS IS THAT SHE PUSHED TOO HARD AND HER POWER ESCAPED HER CONTROL.
"THE HEAT SHE WAS TRYING TO GENERATE EMERGED IN THE WARMEST SPOT IN THE ROOM.
"OUR POOR LAB TECH."
WE'RE HOPING SHE'LL WAKE UP SOON AND BE ABLE TO TELL US HERSELF.
AND IF SHE DOESN'T?

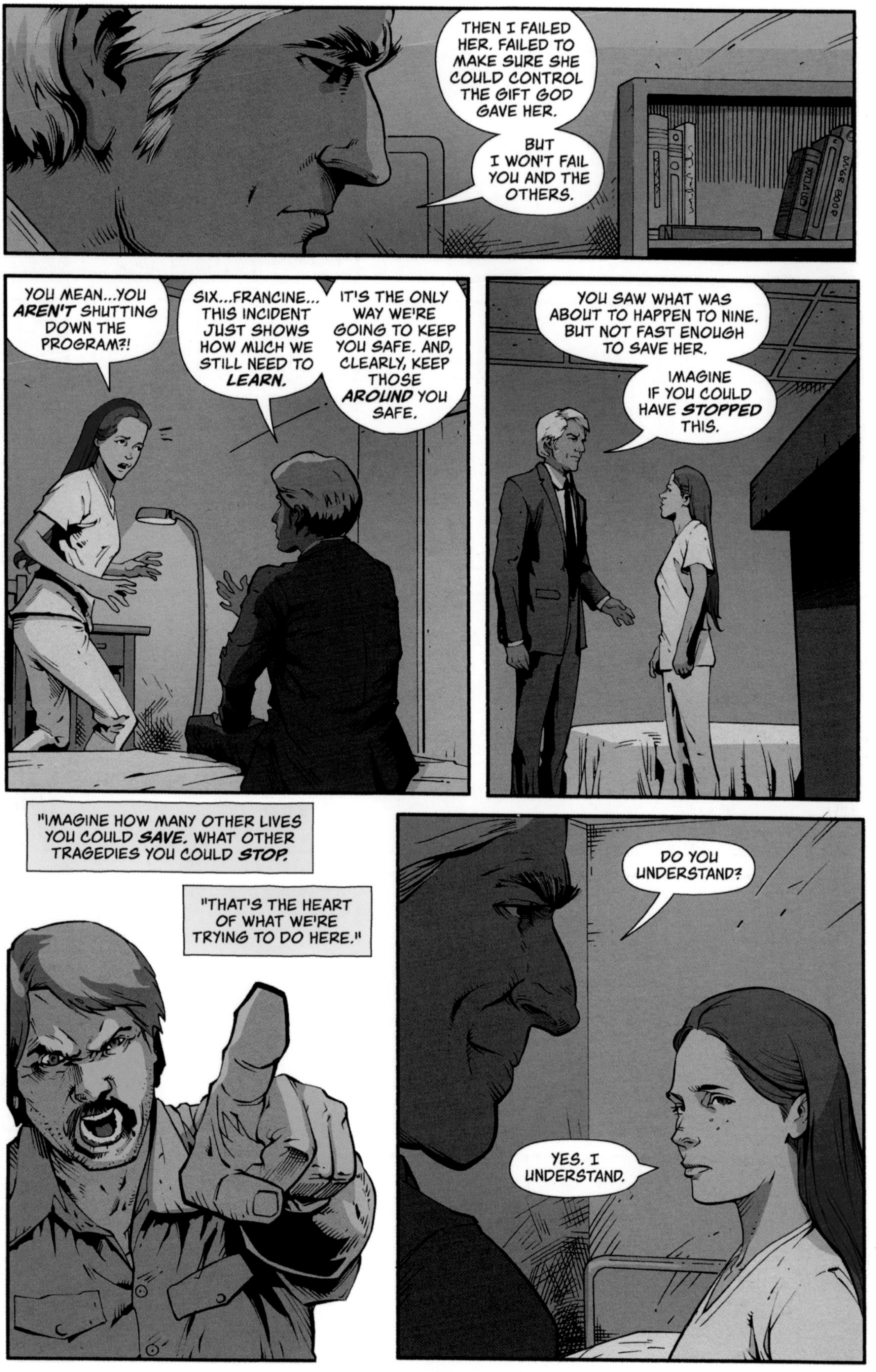
THEN I FAILED HER. FAILED TO MAKE SURE SHE COULD CONTROL THE GIFT GOD GAVE HER.
BUT I WON'T FAIL YOU AND THE OTHERS.
YOU MEAN...YOU AREN'T SHUTTING DOWN THE PROGRAM?!
SIX...FRANCINE... THIS INCIDENT JUST SHOWS HOW MUCH WE STILL NEED TO LEARN.
IT'S THE ONLY WAY WE'RE GOING TO KEEP YOU SAFE. AND, CLEARLY, KEEP THOSE AROUND YOU SAFE.
YOU SAW WHAT WAS ABOUT TO HAPPEN TO NINE. BUT NOT FAST ENOUGH TO SAVE HER.
IMAGINE IF YOU COULD HAVE STOPPED THIS.
"IMAGINE HOW MANY OTHER LIVES YOU COULD SAVE. WHAT OTHER TRAGEDIES YOU COULD STOP.
"THAT'S THE HEART OF WHAT WE'RE TRYING TO DO HERE."
DO YOU UNDERSTAND?
YES. I UNDERSTAND.

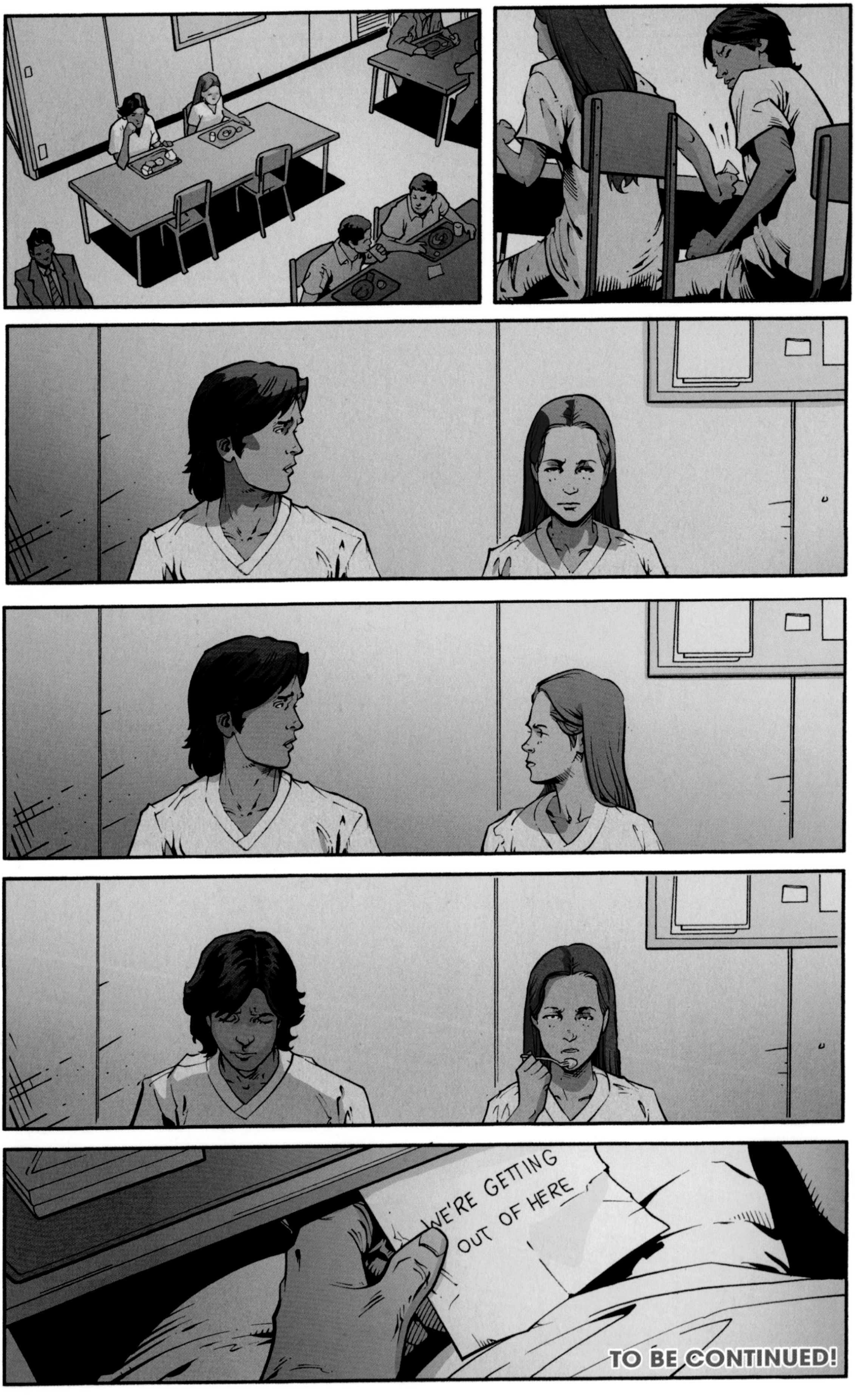
WE'RE GETTING OUT OF HERE
TO BE CONTINUED!